JUV
FIC
LOB   Lobel, Arnold

Small pig

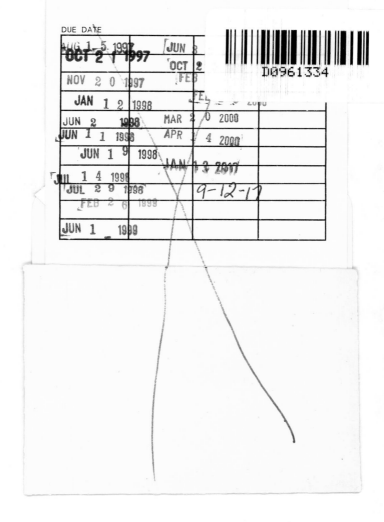

SMALL PIG

Story and Pictures by

Arnold Lobel

An I CAN READ Book®

HarperCollins*Publishers*

I Can Read Book is a registered trademark of
HarperCollins Publishers.

SMALL PIG
Copyright © 1969 by Arnold Lobel.
Library of Congress Catalog Card Number: 69-10213
ISBN 0-06-023932-8 (lib. bdg.)

For Dreamnose

The small pig

lives in a pigpen on a farm.

The small pig likes to eat,

and he likes to run

around the barnyard,

and he likes to sleep.

But most of all

the small pig likes to sit down

and sink down

in good, soft mud.

7

The farmer and his wife
love the small pig.
"We think you are
the best pig in the world,"
they say.

One morning the farmer's wife says,
"Today I will clean my house."

She cleans the upstairs.

Then she cleans the downstairs.

"My house is spotless,"
says the farmer's wife,
"but the rest of this farm
is very dirty.
I will get to work
and clean it up."

The farmer's wife cleans the barn

and the stable

and the chicken coop.

Then she comes to the pigpen.

"Heavens!" cries the farmer's wife.

"This is the dirtiest spot of all."

16

So she cleans the pigpen,

and she washes the pig.

"That's better,"

says the farmer's wife.

"Now everything

is neat and shiny."

18

"Where is my good, soft mud?"

asks the small pig.

"I guess it is gone,"

says the farmer. "I'm sorry."

The small pig

is more than sorry.

He is angry.

"This place is too neat

and shiny for me," he says.

And that night

the small pig runs away.

Soon he finds a swamp.

"Ah!" cries the small pig.

"Here is good, soft mud."

The small pig sits down

and sinks down into the mud.

"Lovely, lovely," he says,

and then he goes to sleep.

"Ouch!" says the small pig

as a dragonfly bumps into his nose.

"Oops!" says the small pig

as a frog jumps onto his head.

"Yow!" says the small pig.

A turtle is biting his tail.

"Move yourself out of here!"

says a big snake.

"You are taking up space

that belongs to us."

So the small pig

moves himself out of there

in a hurry

and runs on down the road.

"Here is a very dirty place,"

says the small pig.

28

"There is sure to be

some good, soft mud nearby."

The small pig

finds broken bottles

and old television sets.

He finds kitchen sinks

and empty soup cans,

but he does not find mud.

30

"Cars are fun," says the small pig,

"but not as much fun as mud."

"Sofas are soft," says the small pig,

"but not as soft as mud."

32

Then he sees something

that he does not like at all.

"That is why there is no mud

around here!" cries the small pig.

And he runs on down the road.

At the end of the road

is a large city.

"Even the air is dirty here,"

says the small pig.

"There is sure to be

some good, soft mud nearby."

34

Soon the small pig

finds what he is looking for.

"Ah!" he says.

"Here is mud."

Then he sits down

and sinks down

into the good, soft mud.

"This mud is strange,"

says the small pig.

"It is not very soft at all.

In fact, it is getting harder

and harder."

He tries to get up,

but he cannot move.

Soon a few people

stop to stare

at the small pig.

40

More and more people

come to see

the small pig.

Then many, many people

come to look

44

because they have never seen

a pig stuck in the sidewalk.

The farmer and his wife

drive by in their car.

"Look at that big crowd

of people," says the farmer.

"Let's stop and see

what is happening."

"All right," says the farmer's wife,

"but hurry.

We must keep looking for

our lost pig."

The farmer stops the car.

"What is happening here?"

he asks a man.

"Oh, nothing much,"

says the man.

"There is just a pig

stuck in the sidewalk."

48

"Heavens!"

cries the farmer's wife.

"That is OUR pig

that's stuck in the sidewalk!"

"Call the police!

Call the firemen!"

shouts the farmer.

By this time
everyone
in the city
has come to see
the small pig.
The policemen
hold back
the huge crowd.

The firemen bring tools

to break the sidewalk.

"Please," says the farmer's wife,
"be very careful.
We think that pig
is the best
in the world."

The firemen work very carefully,

and soon

the small pig is free.

He jumps into the arms

of the farmer and his wife.

They all drive home together.

Just as they come to the farm

the sky turns dark,

and a storm begins.

It rains and rains.

The farmer says, "Look!

Now there is a brand new

mud puddle in the pigpen."

The farmer's wife says,

"And I promise

never to clean it up again."

So the small pig

runs into the pigpen.

First he has his supper.

62

Then he sits down

and sinks down

into the good, soft mud.

THE END